# The Blind Pony

# Do you love ponies? Be a Pony Pal!

Look for these Pony Pal books:

#1   I Want a Pony

#2   A Pony for Keeps

#3   A Pony in Trouble

#4   Give Me Back My Pony

#5   Pony to the Rescue

#6   Too Many Ponies

#7   Runaway Pony

#8   Good-bye Pony

#9   The Wild Pony

  Super Special #1   The Baby Pony

#10   Don't Hurt My Pony

#11   Circus Pony

#12   Keep Out, Pony!

#13   The Girl Who Hated Ponies

#14   Pony-Sitters

  Super Special #2   The Story of Our Ponies
  *coming soon*

#16   The Missing Pony Pal

# PONY PALS

## The Blind Pony

### Jeanne Betancourt

#### illustrated by Paul Bachem

A
**LITTLE APPLE**
PAPERBACK

SCHOLASTIC INC.
New York Toronto London Auckland Sydney

ISBN 0-590-86632-X

24 23 22 21 20 19 18 17 16 15 14 13          3 4 5 6 7 8 9/0

Printed in the U.S.A.                                              40

First Scholastic printing, July 1997

Thank you to Linda Bushnell of Fair Weather Farm, Dr. Kent Kay, Dr. Kate Kane, and Jim Conway of Thistledown Farm.

# Contents

1. Two Strangers 1
2. A Short Trail Ride 10
3. Barn Sleepover 18
4. The Hiding Bush 25
5. The Sneeze 32
6. Three Ideas 39
7. Visit to the Vet 46
8. More Bad News 54
9. The Wrights Are Wrong 61
10. The Perfect Pony 68

# The Blind Pony

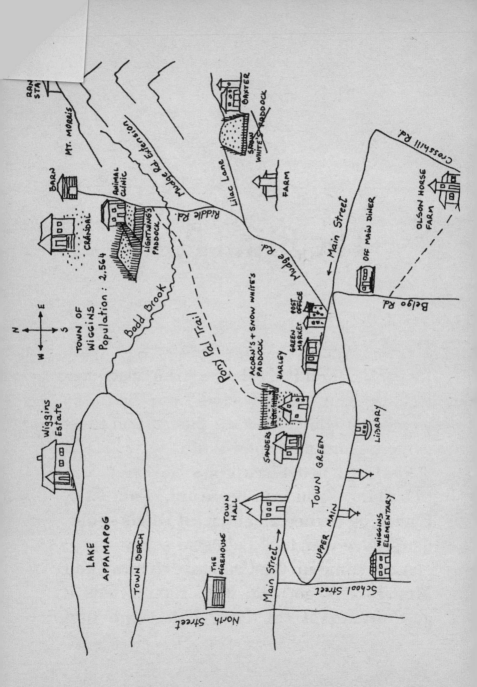

# Two Strangers

Pam Crandal was grooming her pony Lightning for a Pony Pal trail ride. Soon her friends, Anna Harley and Lulu Sanders, would be galloping across the field on their ponies, Acorn and Snow White.

Pam brushed Lightning's chestnut coat to a shine. "You look beautiful," Pam said. Lightning turned and nuzzled Pam's shoulder. "I love you, too," Pam said softly.

A car came up the Crandal driveway and Mrs. Baxter got out. Mrs. Baxter was a good friend of the Pony Pals. Pam and

Lightning went over to the paddock fence to talk to her.

"Will you and your friends do me a favor?" Mrs. Baxter asked.

"Sure," said Pam. Mrs. Baxter had helped the Pony Pals a lot. Pam was glad they could do something for her for a change.

"I sold the Kennedy property on Mudge Road," Mrs. Baxter said. "And the new owners' granddaughter is visiting for a month. Her name is Kim Wright."

Pam smiled. "I bet you want us to be friends with Kim," she said.

"You guessed it," said Mrs. Baxter. "I told her all about the Pony Pals. Kim is your age. But there's something else she has in common with you."

"She has a pony?!" exclaimed Pam.

"That's right," said Mrs. Baxter. "And he's a darling pony." Mrs. Baxter scratched Lightning's upside-down heart and Lightning whickered happily. "The Wrights told me that Kim is an excellent rider."

"I'll tell Lulu and Anna and we'll go see her today," said Pam.

After Mrs. Baxter left, Pam saddled up Lightning. As she was tightening the girth, she saw Anna and Lulu riding across the field. Pam mounted Lightning and rode out to meet them. She couldn't wait to tell them about the new girl and her pony.

"Let's invite her to go trail riding with us today," said Anna.

"We can take her on the trails on the Wiggins Estate," added Lulu. "There are so many neat trails there."

"Let's go!" said Pam.

The Pony Pals rode down Riddle Road and along Mudge Road. Lightning turned her head and nickered softly as if to say, "Look at that." Pam looked. She saw a girl riding a small, dark brown pony around a fenced-in field. Pam knew that the field belonged to the Wrights. The girl must be Kim.

Pam pointed to the girl and her pony. "There she is," she told Anna and Lulu.

The Pony Pals rode up to the fence and waved to Kim.

Kim didn't wave back. She kept riding around the field.

"Why doesn't she come over?" asked Anna.

"Maybe she's shy," said Lulu.

"Maybe she didn't see us," said Pam. She waved again and shouted, "Hi! We're friends of Mrs. Baxter."

"She told you about us," yelled Anna.

"We came over to meet you and your pony," added Lulu.

Kim dismounted and led her pony slowly across the big field.

"Why doesn't she just ride up to us?" asked Lulu.

"It would be a lot faster," said Anna.

"It is strange, isn't it?" said Pam.

Kim and her pony came to a jump rail lying in the field. Pam noticed something else that surprised her. Kim led the pony around the rail.

I would have let Lightning step over the rail, thought Pam.

Kim was small, like Anna, and had long, straight dark hair. Her brown pony was very cute.

The Pony Pals introduced themselves and their ponies to Kim.

"What's your pony's name?" Anna asked her.

"His name is Dandy," said Kim.

"He looks like a Dartmoor pony," said Pam.

"He is," said Kim.

Pam wanted to reach out and pet Dandy. But Kim kept him too far from the fence for petting or for making friends with the other ponies.

"Are those your grandparents?" asked Anna.

A man and woman were walking across the field and waving to the Pony Pals. "Hello! Hello!" they called cheerfully.

Kim nodded.

The Pony Pals introduced themselves to Mr. and Mrs. Wright.

"Mrs. Baxter said such nice things about you girls," said Mrs. Wright. "And you all have such pretty ponies."

Mr. Wright patted Dandy on the nose. The pony shied.

"Sorry, Dandy," said Mr. Wright. "I thought you saw me coming at you."

"He was looking at me," said Kim.

But Pam knew that Dandy was looking right at Mr. Wright the whole time. She wondered why Kim had lied.

"Dandy and Kim have won a lot of blue ribbons," said Mrs. Wright. "And he's great for trail riding, too."

"Kim, tell them about that long trail ride you and your parents went on," said Mr. Wright.

"It was no big deal," said Kim.

"Sure it was," said Kim's grandmother. "Your mother and father said Dandy was better than their fancy horses."

Kim shifted from one foot to the other and looked at the ground. She didn't seem to want to talk about her pony.

"Do you want to come on a trail ride with us?" Pam asked Kim.

"I can't," said Kim. "I have to study."

"How come you have homework in the summer?" asked Anna.

"Kim is doing a math workbook and studying French during her vacation," Mrs. Wright explained to the Pony Pals. "She even has a French tutor while she's here."

"Her parents feel it's important for her to learn another language," said Mr. Wright. He put his arm around Kim's shoulder. "You can study later," he told her. "It's a beautiful day. You should go riding with your new friends."

Kim sighed. "Okay, Grandpa," she said softly. "If you want me to."

"You three bring your ponies up to the house," Mr. Wright told the Pony Pals. "We'll meet you there."

Kim and Dandy followed her grandparents across the field.

"Kim wasn't very friendly," said Lulu.

"Why did you invite her to ride with us, Pam?" asked Anna. "She's such a snob."

"I told Mrs. Baxter we'd be friends with her," said Pam.

"I still wish we didn't have to ride with her," Anna said.

"She's not going to be any fun," added Lulu.

Pam knew that her friends were unhappy that she invited Kim to ride with them. She hoped it wasn't a mistake.

## A Short Trail Ride

The Pony Pals walked their ponies along Mudge Road and up the Wrights' driveway.

"Maybe Kim will be friendlier when she's riding with us," Pam told Lulu and Anna. "Let's be extra nice to her."

"It won't be easy," said Anna. "But I'll try."

"Me too," sighed Lulu.

Kim and her grandparents were waiting for the Pony Pals in front of the house.

"We're going to take you on some great trails," Anna told Kim cheerfully.

"There's a big field where we practice jumping," added Lulu.

"I want to go on the trail behind the house," said Kim.

"You and Dandy go there all the time, Kim," said her grandfather. "Why don't you let these girls show you something new?"

"I don't want to go anyplace new today," said Kim.

Lightning pulled on his lead to get closer to Dandy. Pam knew her pony wanted to make friends with Dandy. But Kim yanked her pony away from Lightning. She wouldn't let her pony be friendly!

"Okay, we can go on your trail," Lulu told Kim.

"You can take the lead, Kim," said Anna.

"I want to go last," said Kim.

"Whatever you want, Kim," said Anna. Anna rolled her eyes at Pam. Pam knew that Anna hated people who always had to have their own way.

The four girls rode their ponies onto the

trail. Anna took the lead followed by Lulu, Pam, and Kim.

Pam remembered when Lulu was the new girl in town. Lulu had lived in exciting, faraway places with her father. Lulu's mother died when she was little, so it was just Lulu and her dad. Her father studied wild animals and Lulu loved traveling with him. She was always ready for a new adventure. When Lulu turned ten, her dad decided that she should stay in one place for awhile. That's when Lulu came to Wiggins to live with her Grandmother Sanders.

At first Lulu thought Wiggins would be boring. She changed her mind when she met Pam and Anna and became a Pony Pal.

Pam and Anna had been best friends since they were five years old. Pam thought that anyone who met Anna Harley would want to be her friend. Anna had loads of energy and always had good ideas about how to have fun. She loved animals and the outdoors. One big thing that Anna didn't like was school. Anna was dyslexic, so reading and writing were hard for her. But drawing came easy. She was a terrific artist.

Pam liked school. And, like Anna and Lulu, she loved ponies. Pam's mother was a riding teacher and her father was a veterinarian. So Pam had been around animals all her life.

The trail behind the Wrights' house was easy, so Pam had plenty of time to think. She wondered why Kim would want to ride such a boring trail over and over again. And why wouldn't she let Pam and Lightning get close to Dandy?

Pam turned to check on Kim and her pony. They were far behind the rest of them.

"I'll wait for you," Pam called back to Kim.

"Don't," said Kim. "Keep going. We're taking our time."

Just then, Dandy bumped into a hanging tree branch. The other ponies had gone

around the branch. Kim said something to Dandy that Pam couldn't hear. Dandy smelled the branch and felt it with his nose. Slowly, Kim backed Dandy up and rode him toward the branch again. This time Dandy walked around it.

Kim saw that Pam was watching them. "What are you staring at?" she yelled angrily. "Go ahead. We'll catch up."

At the end of the trail the Pony Pals waited for Dandy and Kim.

"Isn't this a nice trail?" Kim said cheerfully.

"It is a nice trail," said Anna. She pointed into the woods. "Let's keep riding. If we go that way through the woods we'll come to Lilac Lane. From there we can take a trail to old Ridley Farm."

"It's really neat in there," said Lulu.

"I have to go back," said Kim.

Anna sighed.

"Okay," said Lulu. "If that's what *you* want, I guess that's what we'll do."

Riding back, Pam kept an eye on Kim.

Kim kept talking to Dandy as she rode along. Once Pam heard Kim tell Dandy, "There's a turn coming up."

Kim and the Pony Pals reached the end of the trail and they all dismounted. Pam wondered if Kim would invite them to stay. She didn't. "Thanks for riding with me," she said. "I have to study now."

Pam moved closer to Dandy. "Is something wrong with Dandy's eyes?" she asked.

Kim stood in front of her pony. "He can see fine," she said. She glared at Pam. "There's nothing wrong with him."

Pam backed away. "Okay," she said. "I just asked."

Kim put on a phony smile. "Thanks for riding with me," she said. "Maybe we can get together again sometime."

"Sure," said Lulu. But Lulu wasn't smiling.

"Have fun studying," said Anna. Anna wasn't smiling either.

"Thanks for riding with us," said Pam. "I'll call you."

The Pony Pals mounted and rode away from Kim and her pony.

"Pam, I can't believe you're being so nice to her," said Lulu.

"She was really mean to you," said Anna.

"I think she's upset about Dandy," said Pam. "I think something is wrong with that pony. And I think we should find out what it is."

# Barn Sleepover

The Pony Pals rode single file toward Ridley Farm. When they came to a wide part of the trail, they went side by side.

"I'm glad Kim didn't come with us," said Anna. "She would have ruined everything."

"I don't think that Dandy could ride on these trails anyway," said Pam.

"Why do you think something is wrong with Dandy's eyes?" Lulu asked Pam.

"He bumped into the limb of a tree," said Pam. "And Kim talks to him all the time.

She tells him everything about the trail. Like where there's a turn."

"Maybe he's just clumsy," Anna said.

"Our ponies saw the tree," said Pam. "Dandy should have seen it, too."

"Why doesn't Kim tell us if something is wrong?" asked Anna.

"I don't know," said Pam. "Let's invite her and Dandy to our barn sleepover tonight." "She'll get to know us better. Maybe then she'll tell us what's wrong with Dandy."

"That's a great idea," said Lulu.

"She won't want to come," said Anna. "I don't think she likes us."

"Her grandparents will make her," said Pam. "They want her to have friends in Wiggins."

The Pony Pals rode back to the Crandals' barn and Pam telephoned the Wright house. Kim's grandmother answered the phone. Pam told her that the Pony Pals were inviting Kim and Dandy for a barn sleepover.

"That's very sweet of you," said Mrs. Wright. "I'm sure Kim would love to come."

Mrs. Wright went to get Kim. Pam could hear that Kim didn't want to come for a sleepover. But her Grandmother told her that she should. Finally Kim got on the phone. "Okay, I'll come," she said.

"Great," Pam told Kim. "We have an extra sleeping bag you can use. And Dandy can sleep in the paddock with our ponies."

"Dandy doesn't like other ponies," said Kim. "Besides, he likes to sleep inside."

"We have an extra stall in our barn," said Pam. "He can stay there."

Pam said goodbye and hung up the phone. "Kim and Dandy are coming," she told her friends.

"I suppose we'll have to be nice to her again," said Anna.

"Maybe her pony is going blind," said Pam. "If he is, she'll need Pony Pal help."

"You're right," said Anna. "We should give her another chance."

The Pony Pals went up to the house and

made a picnic supper for the barn sleepover. Then they sat on the paddock fence to wait for Kim and Dandy.

Anna pointed to the road. "Here they come," she said.

Pam saw Kim leading Dandy up Riddle Road.

"She isn't riding him," said Lulu.

The Pony Pals jumped down from the fence and ran to meet Kim. Kim wanted to put Dandy in his stall right away. Pam brought them into the barn and led them to Dandy's stall.

Kim showed Dandy all around the stall. Then she carefully led him through the narrow door to the little corral. She talked to him the whole time. Pam thought, I'd never have to do that with Lightning. He'd get used to a new stall just by seeing it.

Kim left Dandy in the stall and went back outside with Pam.

"Do you want to see the rest of the barn and my Dad's animal hospital?" Pam asked Kim.

"Sure," said Kim. Kim was interested in everything. And she loved meeting the ponies and horses in Mrs. Crandal's riding school. She told the Pony Pals about the thoroughbred horses that her parents owned. "My dad is always looking for the perfect horse," she said. "He and my Mom like everything to be perfect."

"Did they pick out Dandy?" asked Pam.

"We all did," said Kim. "They liked him because he's registered and has an excellent standing in the Dartmoor Pony Society. I don't care about any of that. I just love him because he's so sweet and loving. He has a great personality."

"That's the way I feel about Lightning," said Pam.

The four girls had their picnic supper on a big flat rock near the paddock. Kim told a whole bunch of elephant jokes. Then Pam told eleven knock-knock jokes. The girls laughed until tears rolled down their cheeks.

After supper, the Pony Pals and Kim

went up to the hayloft and Kim taught them a new card game. At ten o'clock, the four girls went down to the barn office. When they were all in their sleeping bags they talked about their ponies. Kim talked about Dandy, but she didn't say anything about his eyesight. Finally, one by one, the girls fell asleep. All except Pam.

Pam lay awake thinking about Kim and Dandy. She slid silently from her sleeping bag and tiptoed out of the barn office. She had to know for sure if Dandy was blind.

# The Hiding Bush

Dandy was in the small paddock outside his stall. Lightning was on the other side of the fence, but next to Dandy. The two ponies were sleeping standing up.

Pam gently stroked Dandy's face. "Wake up, Dandy," she said.

Dandy woke up.

Lightning woke up, too. "I'm glad you made a new friend," Pam told her pony.

Pam put a halter on Dandy and led him into the stall. He bumped into the side of the doorway. Lightning would have seen the doorway, thought Pam.

She moved her hand in front of Dandy's eyes. His eyes didn't follow her hand.

Next, Pam dropped a rolled-up leg wrap in front of Dandy's face. He didn't notice it. Pam knew for sure that the pony couldn't see. Dandy was a blind pony. She patted him on the head. "Poor Dandy," she said softly.

"What are you doing to my pony?" a girl's voice shouted angrily. Kim rushed into the stall. "Get away from my pony!"

Kim threw her arms around Dandy's neck. He rubbed his cheek against her hair. Tears of anger filled her eyes. "What are you doing to my pony?" Kim asked.

"Kim, I think Dandy is going blind," said Pam. "I gave him some tests to be sure." Pam held up the bright blue leg wrap. "I dropped this in front of his face and —"

Kim interrupted Pam. "He can see fine," she said. "He's in a new place. That's confusing for a pony. Besides, he was sleeping and you woke him up."

"Kim, I know he is blind," said Pam. "You know it, too."

"I don't want to talk about it," said Kim. "Ever. And don't tell anyone. Especially Lulu and Anna. It's my secret." She hugged Dandy. "It's *our* secret. Promise me you won't tell anyone."

"I won't tell anyone if you don't want me to," said Pam. "But I think the Pony Pals could help you and Dandy."

"We don't need any help," said Kim. "As long as you keep our secret. You can't tell Anna and Lulu. Promise."

Pam looked at Kim and saw how scared she looked.

"I promise," said Pam.

Pam and Kim quietly went back to the barn office and crawled into their sleeping bags. Pam stayed awake for a long time. She was worried about Dandy. Pam was unhappy. She had never kept a secret from her Pony Pals before. Pam didn't want to have a secret from them now.

When the Pony Pals woke up the next morning Kim wasn't in her sleeping bag.

"Maybe she's with Dandy," said Lulu.

The three friends ran down the barn aisle to the stall. Kim and Dandy were gone. Kim had left them a note. Pam read it aloud.

Dear Pam, Anna, and Lulu,
   Thank you for the good time.
I went home to study.
                Kim

"She didn't have to leave so early," said Lulu. "She could have stayed for breakfast."

"She didn't even say good-bye to us," said Anna.

"We had such a great time last night," said Lulu. "Why'd she leave like that?"

Pam knew why Kim had left. But she didn't tell Anna and Lulu. She kept her promise to Kim.

The Pony Pals got dressed and went out to the paddock to feed their ponies. Lightning was standing at Dandy's paddock fence. Lightning is looking for her new friend, thought Pam.

Anna and Lulu were still talking about Kim while they ate breakfast.

"I think she acted weird," said Lulu. "Nobody leaves a sleepover when everyone else is asleep?"

"Maybe it has something to do with Dandy," said Anna. She turned to Pam. "Remember you said something might be wrong with his eyes?"

"Let's go find her and talk about it," said Lulu.

"Maybe we should leave her alone," said Pam.

"I thought you wanted to help her, Pam," said Anna. "And be her friend."

"I do," said Pam.

"Then let's go," said Lulu.

After breakfast, the Pony Pals walked down Riddle Road to Mudge Road. They saw Kim leading Dandy into the Wrights' big field.

"Let's spy on her," said Anna. "Maybe we can find out for sure if Dandy's blind."

"Good idea," said Lulu.

"I don't think we should spy," said Pam.

"But we want to help her," said Anna. "And she won't tell us herself. We have to find out for sure if he's blind."

Pam still didn't tell her friends that she already knew that Dandy was blind.

Anna pointed to a big bush in the far corner of the field. "Let's hide behind there," she said.

"Perfect," said Lulu.

Lulu and Anna crawled over to the bush and hid behind it. Pam followed them.

Pam peeked through the leaves of the bush. She saw Kim leading Dandy into the field. Kim looked unhappy and worried. Pam wished Kim would tell Anne and Lulu the truth about Dandy. She knew that they would want to help. How could she keep such a big secret from her friends?

# The Sneeze

The Pony Pals were squatting behind the hiding bush and spying on Kim and Dandy through the leaves.

Kim led Dandy to a hay bale. "Here's a big bale of hay, Dandy," Kim told her pony. Dandy smelled the hay and felt it with his nose.

Next, Kim led Dandy back to the gate and mounted. She rode her pony slowly around the field. When they came to the bale of hay, Kim said, "Here's that hay bale. I know you can't see it, but it's there."

Anna and Lulu looked at one another and nodded sadly. Now they knew for sure that Dandy was blind.

Kim turned Dandy at the corner of the field. They rode toward the bush where the Pony Pals were hiding. They came so close that Pam could see the buckles on Dandy's bridle. Just then, Dandy stopped, nodded his head toward the bush, and nickered. A sneeze tickled Pam's nose. She tried to hold her breath.

"That's just a bush," Kim told Dandy. "I'll show it to you."

The Pony Pals looked at one another in alarm. Should they run? Kim would see them for sure if they did. They crouched as low as they could.

Kim and Dandy came right up to the bush. "Smell it," Kim told him. "Feel it with your nose."

Dandy stuck his head in the bush.

Pam sneezed.

Kim screamed.

Dandy shied.

And the Pony Pals came out of hiding.

Kim dismounted and held tight to Dandy's reins. "You scared us," she said. Her voice was shaking. "What . . . what are you doing here?"

"We were —" Pam started to say.

Kim interrupted her. "I know what you were doing!" she said angrily. "You were spying on me!"

"We wanted to find out if Dandy's blind," said Lulu.

"We're sorry that your pony is blind," added Anna.

Kim glared at Pam. "You promised," she said.

"I didn't tell them," said Pam. "They figured it out themselves."

"We want to be your friends," said Anna.

"We want to help you and Dandy," added Lulu.

Kim started to cry. Pam took Dandy's lead rope from Kim. Anna put her arm around Kim's shoulder. And Lulu gave Kim a tissue.

"Let us help you, Kim," said Pam.

The four girls sat down next to the hay bale while Dandy grazed nearby.

Kim wiped her eyes with the tissue and blew her nose. "I didn't want anyone to know Dandy is blind," she said.

"Why is it a secret?" asked Anna.

"Because of my parents," said Kim. "They want me to be in shows and win ribbons. Like they always do. They won't let me keep a pony that can't see."

"*They* must know Dandy is blind," said Anna.

"You couldn't tell at first," said Kim. "It happened slowly. He adjusted all by himself. He's so smart."

"And he knew his home paddock and barn by heart," said Pam.

"But when you came here everything was new to him," said Lulu.

"And now I think he's all the way blind," said Kim. "I'm supposed to be in a big horse show when I go home." Kim started crying all over again. "My parents think I'm here practicing my jumps. They'll never let me keep a blind pony."

Pam felt like crying, too. But she knew she had to stay calm if they were going to help Kim. "We'll help you figure out this problem, Kim," said Pam.

"You're not alone anymore," said Anna.

"We're going to think very hard about what you can do," said Lulu.

Pam saw Kim's grandmother walking toward the field. "Here comes your grandmother," she told Kim.

Kim wiped her eyes and waved to her grandmother. "I'm so glad you girls came over to see Kim," Mrs. Wright said. "But Kim, you better come in now. Your French tutor will be here any minute."

"I have to go," Kim told the Pony Pals.

"I have my reading tutor today," said Anna. She smiled at Kim. "I have to study during summer vacation, too."

"We can come back later," Pam told Kim. "*If* you want us to."

"I want you to," said Kim. She turned to

her grandmother. "Can we have a sleepover here, Grandma?" she asked.

"Of course you can," said her grandmother. "I love that you're making friends in Wiggins."

"Will you come?" Kim asked the Pony Pals.

"Sure," said Pam and Lulu in unison.

"That'd be fun," said Anna.

Mrs. Wright went back to the house and the Pony Pals said good-bye to Kim.

"Can we bring our ponies for the sleepover?" asked Anna.

"Okay," said Kim. Dandy nuzzled against Kim. She hugged her pony. "We have friends to help us now," she told her pony. Kim smiled at Pam. "I'm sorry that I yelled at you. Thank you for keeping my secret. I'm glad that the Pony Pals are going to help us."

The Pony Pals said good-bye to Kim and walked back to Mudge Road. Pam wondered if the Pony Pals would be able to help Kim. A blind pony and parents who wanted everything perfect were a big problem. "It's time for three ideas," Pam told Lulu and Anna.

# Three Ideas

At six o'clock that evening, the Pony Pals tied their sleeping bags to the backs of their saddles and rode over to the Wright house. They found Kim waiting near the field. She was standing beside a big green tent.

The Pony Pals waved to Kim and she ran over to them. "My grandmother and I put up the tent," she said. "We can sleep in it."

"That's great," said Pam.

"It'll be so much fun to sleep outdoors," said Anna.

The Pony Pals took the saddles and bridles off their ponies and let them run free in the field.

"Let's see inside the tent," said Anna.

"Bring your sleeping bags," said Kim. "Mine is already there."

The Pony Pals threw their saddlebags over their shoulders and picked up their sleeping bags. The four girls crawled inside the tent. They laid out their sleeping bags side by side and sat on them.

"Let's have a Pony Pal meeting," said Pam. "And talk about Kim's problem."

"We always start by sharing our ideas," Lulu told Kim. "Pam, you go first."

Pam took out a piece of paper and read her idea out loud.

## My father can check Dandy's eyes.

"You should find out why Dandy's blind," said Pam.

"What if he says Dandy should be put to sleep?" said Kim.

"He'll want you to keep your pony," said Anna.

"My father loves all animals," said Pam. "Even if they're not perfect."

"And he might be able to cure him," added Lulu.

"I never thought of that," said Kim. "Can we have him checked tomorrow?"

"I'll call my Dad right after this meeting," said Pam.

"Thanks," said Kim. She turned to Lulu. "What's your idea?"

Lulu handed her idea to Kim. Kim read it out loud.

We can help you train Dandy.

"I think you need help to train a blind pony," said Lulu.

"That would be great," said Kim.

"It'll be good for Dandy to be around people and other ponies," said Pam.

"That's what my idea is about," said Anna. She took a folded piece of paper from her saddlebag and opened it up.

"Even though Dandy is blind, he should be with other ponies," said Anna. "As long as they're ponies he can trust."

"Lightning can help train Dandy, too," said Pam. "She helped us train my mother's school ponies."

"And she helped tame a wild pony," added Lulu.

"Lightning is wonderful with other animals," said Pam. "She protected a litter of kittens once."

Kim jumped up. "Let's put Lightning and Dandy together now."

"Where is Dandy?" asked Pam.

"He's in the little paddock on the other side of the house," said Kim.

"We can put Acorn and Snow White in that paddock," said Lulu. "Then Lightning and Dandy can be in the big field near us."

"Can I bring Dandy over here now?" asked Pam. "He should get used to me."

Kim agreed.

Pam went to the paddock to catch Dandy. Dandy can't see me, she thought. So I have to talk to him a little before I go up to him.

A few minutes later, Pam walked Dandy into the field. Lightning looked up from grazing. When she saw Dandy and Pam she came over to them. Dandy shied back.

"That's your friend Lightning," Kim told Dandy.

Lightning nickered softly at Dandy. Dandy sniffed the air. He took a step forward and sniffed again. He rubbed his nose

along Lightning's neck. And Lightning rubbed Dandy's neck.

"See," Pam whispered to Kim. "I told you they were friends."

Pam unhooked Dandy's lead rope, but she left on his halter. "Just in case we have to catch him," she explained to Kim.

Lightning walked toward the middle of the field. She turned and whinnied at Dandy. Dandy followed her. Soon the two ponies were grazing side by side.

"They look beautiful together," said Kim.

"Lightning will be a good friend to Dandy," said Pam.

"I hope your Dad will be able to cure Dandy's blindness," said Kim.

I hope so, too, thought Pam. But could he? What would happen to Dandy?

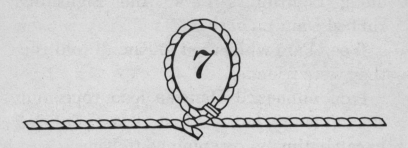

## Visit to the Vet

The next morning, the Pony Pals and Kim led Dandy up Riddle Road. They had a ten o'clock appointment with Pam's father.

Dr. Crandal started the exam by asking Kim some questions about Dandy. After the interview, he listened to Dandy's heart and lungs. He felt Dandy's legs, took his temperature, and looked in his eyes with a penlight. Then Dr. Crandal used an ophthalmoscope to look at the interior of the eyes. Pam liked watching her father at work. She wanted to be a veterinarian someday, too.

Dr. Crandal picked up a leg wrap and dropped it in front of Dandy's face. Pam knew that Dandy would not flinch. She went over to stand next to Kim and watched her dad move his hands in front of Dandy's eyes. Finally, Dr. Crandal led Dandy through the door on a loose lead. Dandy bumped into the gatepost. He was doing all the tests that Pam had done.

"You girls are right," said Dr. Crandal. "This pony is blind."

Pam put her arm around Kim. She knew that Kim was feeling very sad.

Dr. Crandal held up a big needle. "I'm going to take a sample of his blood," he told the girls. "I'll send it to the lab. We need to find out if an infection is hurting Dandy's eyesight."

Kim and Lulu looked away and Anna covered her eyes. But Pam watched the needle go into Dandy's neck. She was used to watching her dad give shots.

"Can you cure him, Dr. Crandal?" asked Kim.

"I won't know until we have the results of the blood work," he said. "If Dandy has an infection, we may be able to help him. If he doesn't have an infection, there is nothing I can do for him."

Dr. Crandal handed Dandy's reins to Kim.

"Dad, when will you know if Dandy has an infection?" asked Pam.

"In twenty-four hours," answered Dr. Crandal. "Come back here at the same time tomorrow."

"Thank you, Dr. Crandal," said Kim.

Pam knew that Kim was worried. As they all walked Dandy back toward the Wrights', Pam put her arm around Kim.

"We still don't know if Dandy can be cured," said Kim.

"But we'll know tomorrow," Pam reminded her. She tried to sound positive.

"Let's work with Dandy now," said Lulu. "Just in case he *can't* be cured."

"That's a good idea," said Kim. She

looked at her watch. "But I have my French tutor in a little while."

"We'll wait for you," said Pam.

"And we'll think about how to train Dandy," added Lulu.

"Thank you for helping me," said Kim.

"We're doing it for Dandy, too," said Anna.

Just then Dandy whinnied at Anna as if to say *Thank you.* Kim and the Pony Pals laughed.

While Kim was with her tutor, the Pony Pals sat under the trees in the apple orchard and talked about Dandy.

"Let's make up some easy exercises for him to do," said Lulu.

"We'll have Lightning do them with him," said Pam.

"That'll be a big help to Dandy," added Anna.

After the girls made up the exercises, they prepared the field for the lesson. They moved a bale of hay and laid jump rails on the ground. When Kim came out, everything was ready for Dandy's lesson.

Pam pointed to the bale of hay. "We want Dandy to learn to walk around it," she told Kim.

"See the rails on the ground?" asked Lulu. "He should learn to step over things when you tell him to."

"He has to trust you even more than he does now," said Anna.

"Let's get started," said Kim.

Kim, the Pony Pals, and Lightning did the exercises with Dandy. Sometimes Lightning went ahead of Dandy and sometimes the two ponies walked side by side. When Dandy made a mistake, Lightning neighed softly as if to say, "That's okay. Try again."

By the end of the day, Dandy went around the bale of hay without bumping into it. And he was learning that when Kim said "UP" he was supposed to step over the fence rails.

That night the four girls had another

barn sleepover. Kim let Dandy sleep outside with Lightning.

At quarter to ten the next morning, the four girls were in Dr. Crandal's office. They watched the clock and waited. At ten o'clock, the fax came with Dandy's blood test results. Pam held her breath while her father read the paper.

Finally, he looked up at Kim and the Pony Pals. "Dandy doesn't have an infection that would cause blindness," he said. "I think he has a tumor on his optic nerve. I can't fix that. I don't think Dandy will ever see again."

"Oh," said Kim softly.

Pam thought Kim would cry, but she didn't.

"I'm sorry, Kim," said Dr. Crandal.

"Me, too," said Lulu.

Pam put her hand on Kim's arm.

"Poor Dandy," said Anna.

"Dandy is doing all right," said Dr. Crandal. "He has his smelling and his hearing."

He smiled at Kim. "And you're his eyes, Kim," he said.

"I know," she said.

"You must love Dandy very much," said Dr. Crandal.

"I do," she said.

"Take him to your own vet when you go home," Dr. Crandal said. "And have the doctor call me." He handed Kim his business card.

The Pony Pals left the office and went out to their ponies. No one spoke. Kim went over to Dandy and hugged him.

Pam imagined how she would feel if Lightning were blind. She knew she would love her more than ever. She also knew that her parents would let her keep a blind pony. But would Kim's parents let Kim keep Dandy?

## More Bad News

"It's time for another Pony Pal meeting," said Lulu.

"Let's go to my mother's diner," said Anna. "We can have lunch *and* a meeting."

Everyone agreed that taking Kim to Off-Main Diner was a great idea. "First, let's take Dandy and Lightning back to Kim's," said Pam. "We can have a lesson with them after lunch."

Everyone agreed to that idea, too.

By noon the four girls were in the Pony Pals' favorite booth in Off-Main Diner. "We have to be our own waiters," Anna explained to Kim. "But we don't have to pay for what we eat."

"Anna's mom owns this place," Pam told Kim.

Lulu wrote down their orders. They all wanted grilled cheese and french fries.

"And brownies for dessert," added Anna.

While the girls waited for their food, they started their Pony Pal meeting. Pam took out her notebook and pencil.

"When do you have to go home?" Lulu asked Kim.

"In three weeks," said Kim.

"We'll work with Dandy every day until then," said Pam.

"You and Dandy will be so good together that your parents will let you keep him," said Anna.

Kim looked discouraged. "They'll take him away from me," she said. "I know they will."

"You can't think that way," said Lulu. "Think about training Dandy."

"Let's make a chart of all the things we want to teach him," said Pam.

"And each time he does something," said Anna, "we'll mark it down."

The girls worked on the chart until the cook yelled, "Pony Pal platters on deck."

They finished the chart after they ate.

| OK = Okay<br>MW = More Work | OK | MW |
|---|---|---|
| Walking around field on loose lead | | |
| Riding around field at walk | | |
| Riding around field at walk with rails and hay bale | | |
| Riding around field at trot | | |
| Trotting around field with rails and hay bale | | |
| Serpentines | | |

That afternoon the Pony Pals and Lightning worked with Kim and Dandy for two hours. The next morning they had another lesson.

In the afternoon, the girls moved the hay bale. Kim mounted Dandy.

"Let him smell and feel the hay bale," said Pam.

Dandy did it. He knew there was a bale of hay in front of him.

"Now back up," said Pam.

Dandy did that.

"When you reach the hay bale this time," said Pam, "say, *around*."

Kim did what Pam said.

But Dandy bumped into the hay bale.

"We'll try it again," said Pam. "Kim, back him up. We're going to do it until we get it right."

Lulu and Anna giggled.

"What's so funny?" asked Pam.

"You sound just like your mother," said Anna.

Pam laughed, too. Sometimes she wanted to be a riding teacher instead of a veterinarian. She wondered if she could be both.

The fifth time that Dandy came to the

hay bale he walked around it without bumping the bale.

The girls clapped and Lightning whinnied.

Every day that week the Pony Pals rode their ponies over to the Wright house.

Snow White and Acorn stayed in the small paddock during Dandy's lessons. But after the lessons all the ponies grazed together in the big field.

On the fifth morning of lessons, Kim met the Pony Pals on Riddle Road. Pam saw her running toward them.

"There's Kim," said Lulu.

"I really like her," said Anna.

"She's great," said Lulu.

If Kim lived in Wiggins, thought Pam, there would be four Pony Pals.

Kim was breathless when she reached the Pony Pals. Pam saw that she'd been crying.

"What's wrong?" asked Pam.

"My . . . my . . . parents are coming to get me," she said. "Today."

"What?!" exclaimed Anna and Lulu together.

"Why?" asked Pam.

"My mother found a new riding teacher to work with me and Dandy," she said. "To improve our jumps. She and my dad want to be sure we're ready for the big horse show next month."

"Did you tell them about Dandy?" asked Lulu.

Kim shook her head no.

"We'll help you tell them," said Pam.

"They have to let you keep Dandy," said Anna. "He is such a wonderful pony."

"He is," said Pam. But she knew that Kim's parents wouldn't want their daughter to have a blind pony. Even a pony as wonderful as Dandy.

# The Wrights Are Wrong

"What time will your parents get here?" Pam asked Kim.

Kim looked at her watch. "In about an hour," she said.

"Time enough to practice," said Pam. "Let's go."

Kim ran beside Pam and Lightning. When they reached the Wrights' they quickly groomed Dandy and put on his tack. Kim led him to the gate to begin the exercise. Lightning nudged Pam and neighed as if to say, "Let's start."

Kim and the Pony Pals laughed. Lightning wanted to help with the lesson. Pam brought Lightning up beside Dandy. Pam and Kim mounted their ponies, and the lesson began.

Dandy took the lead and they walked around the field. Dandy's ears were back and he listened to Kim. She told him "around" when they came to the hay bale and he went around it. She said "up" when they came to the rails and he stepped over them. Pam and Lightning followed.

Anna and Lulu moved the rails and bale of hay. The two riders and ponies circled the field again. They went around the hay bale, but Dandy tripped on one of the rails.

"Let's take a break," said Pam. "Then we'll try it again."

Kim and Pam dismounted and led their ponies to the water trough.

"Hey, there," called a man's voice.

Pam saw a man and woman walking across the field with Kim's grandmother.

"Kim!" shouted the woman excitedly.

Kim ran over to her parents. The Pony Pals followed with Lightning and Dandy.

"These are Kim's new friends," said Kim's grandmother.

Kim introduced each of the Pony Pals to her parents.

"Hello," said Kim's father.

"It's a pleasure to meet you," said Kim's mother.

Kim's mother said something to Kim in French and Kim answered in French.

*"Très bien,"* said Kim's mother. Pam knew that *très bien* was French for "very good."

"So you have been studying your French," said Kim's father. "And how's the math coming along?"

"Good," said Kim. "I'm doing all the work you gave me."

"And have you been working with Dandy every day, too?" asked her mother.

"Twice a day," said Kim.

"The Pony Pals have been helping her," said Kim's grandmother.

"We were disappointed in Dandy's performance at the shows this spring," Kim's mother told the Pony Pals.

"Those girls are out here with Dandy all day long," said Kim's grandmother.

"Except when Kim's studying," added Pam.

"So Dandy's jumping must be improving," said Kim's father.

"He's not jumping much right now," said Kim.

"That's what I was afraid of," scolded her father. "Well, your new riding teacher will take care of that. She'll have you flying over the jumps. You and Dandy will be winning first prizes again."

"Dandy doesn't jump anymore," said Kim.

"Why not?" asked her father sternly.

Kim looked at Pam. Pam nodded. It was time for Kim to tell her parents the truth.

Kim put her arm around Dandy's neck. He nickered softly. "Dandy doesn't jump anymore," said Kim, "because he's blind."

"Blind!" exclaimed Kim's father.

"What do you mean?" asked Kim's mother.

"I mean he can't see," said Kim. "And he can't be cured."

"My father's a veterinarian," said Pam. "He examined him."

Kim's father turned to her grandmother. "Mother, did you know about this?" he asked.

"Dr. Crandal called me after he examined the pony," she said. "Kim said she wanted to tell you herself. It's very sad, but the Pony Pals have been so lovely. They've helped Kim and Dandy."

Kim's father's face was turning red with anger. "A blind pony!" he said. "We've only had him a year. Carl Simpson will have to take him back and refund our money."

"It's not Mr. Simpson's fault," said Kim. "Dandy was all right when we bought him."

"Carl will have to take him back anyway," said Mr. Wright. "Dandy's useless. Let Carl get rid of him."

Kim burst into tears.

Her mother put her arm around her shoulder. "Don't cry, sweetie," she said. "We'll buy you another pony. One that's perfect. My little girl is going to have a perfect pony."

"Dandy is perfect," sobbed Kim. "I want to keep Dandy."

"Keep him?!" said Kim's mother. "But he's blind, dear."

"We're not keeping a blind pony," said Kim's father. "And that is that."

The Pony Pals exchanged a look. They had to think of a way to help Kim. And *fast*.

## The Perfect Pony

"I want to keep Dandy," sobbed Kim.

"A blind pony is useless," said her father.

"Dandy isn't useless!" said Kim. Kim wasn't crying anymore. Now she was angry.

"What's anyone supposed to do with a blind pony?" asked Kim's father.

"Take care of him," said Pam.

"Be his friend," said Lulu.

"And love him," said Anna.

"You can't show with a blind pony," said Kim's father.

"Winning ribbons isn't as important as loving your pony," said Kim.

Kim's father glared at Pam. "I bet your father said he should be put down," he said.

"No, he didn't," said a man's voice.

Pam saw her father walking toward the group around Dandy. The pony turned his head and whinnied softly at Dr. Crandal.

"Who are *you*?" asked Kim's father.

"I'm Dr. Robert Crandal," Dr. Crandal said. "Pam's father." He extended his hand to shake with Kim's father. "I'm sorry about your pony." He nodded at Kim's grandmother. "Your mother called to tell me you were coming. I thought I should speak to you myself."

"I'm John Wright," said Kim's father. "The fool who bought a blind pony."

"And I'm Laura Thompson Wright," said Kim's mother. "We're glad to meet you. We've had a bit of a shock here."

"They said I have to give Dandy back," Kim told Dr. Crandal. "And that he'll be put to sleep."

"Just what's happened to Dandy, Doctor?" asked Kim's father.

"It looks like a tumor grew on his optic nerve," said Dr. Crandal. "It isn't something you can operate on."

"So he's blind for life?" said Kim's mother.

"I'm afraid so," Dr. Crandal said. "But that doesn't mean his life is over. Dandy is a very special pony. And your daughter knows how to handle him." Dr. Crandal smiled at Kim. "You should be proud of both of them."

"What Kim is doing with Dandy is worth a lot more than a bunch of ribbons," said Lulu.

"Dandy trots all around the field," said Anna. "And goes around the hay bale."

Pam whispered to Kim, "Show them."

"You mean you've been riding a blind pony?" Kim's father asked.

"Watch," said Kim. She led Dandy to the gate and mounted him.

Lightning nudged Pam. She wanted to

ride with her friend. "Not this time," Pam whispered to Lightning.

Kim's mother and father stood side by side. "Do you think it's safe?" Kim's mother asked Kim's father.

"I don't think much is going to happen," he said. "What can she do on a blind pony?"

Pam noticed that Anna had her fingers crossed behind her back. Pam rubbed Lightning's upside-down heart and wished good luck for Kim and Dandy.

Kim rode Dandy around the hay bale and over the rails. He did it all perfectly.

"That's amazing," said Kim's mother. She turned to Dr. Crandal. "Are you sure he's blind?"

"He can't see a thing," said Dr. Crandal.

"He must have memorized where everything is," Kim's father said.

"Kim," shouted Pam. "Go back to the gate. We'll move things around."

Pam moved the hay bale while Lulu and Anna moved the rails.

Kim and Dandy went around the field

twice more. Once at a walk and once at a trot. The blind pony didn't bump into the hay bale. He didn't trip on the rails.

Everyone applauded.

"Wonderful!" exclaimed Kim's father.

"He was perfect!" exclaimed Lulu.

"A perfect pony," said Anna.

Kim dismounted and led Dandy back to them.

"How does he know where those things are?" Kim's father asked.

"Kim trained him," Pam said. "He trusts her and he listens to her."

Pam saw that Kim's mother's eyes were filled with tears. "I'm so proud of you," she told Kim.

"I want to keep Dandy," Kim told her parents. "I'm his eyes. As long as he's with me he's not really blind."

"How can you be Dandy's eyes and be a top student?" asked Kim's father.

"I'll keep my grades up," said Kim. "I can do both. I promise."

"What about horse shows?" asked Kim's mother.

"I don't care about horse shows," said Kim. "I care about Dandy."

"We could try it," Kim's father said to her mother.

"I think we should," said Kim's mother.

"Okay," said Kim's father.

Kim dismounted. She hugged her blind pony. Then she hugged her parents.

The Pony Pals raised their hands and hit high fives. "All *right!*" they shouted.

Kim stood with the Pony Pals. Pam noticed that she looked sad.

"Kim, what's wrong?" asked Pam.

"Aren't you happy?" asked Lulu.

"You can keep Dandy," said Anna.

"I'm sad because I have to leave Wiggins," said Kim. "I'll miss the Pony Pals."

Kim's grandmother put her arm around Kim's shoulder and gave her a squeeze. "You and that darling pony will be back," she said.

"That's right," said Kim with a smile. "I'll visit lots."

The Pony Pals raised their right hands again. This time Kim joined them. "All *right!*" they shouted.

"All *right* for the Wrights!" shouted Anna.

"Would you look at that!" said Kim's mother. She pointed to Dandy and Lightning. They were rubbing noses.

Pam felt great. She was proud of her pony and of her Pony Pals.

They had all helped Kim keep her blind pony.

Dear Reader:

I am having a lot of fun researching and writing books about the Pony Pals. I've met many interesting kids and adults who love ponies. And I've visited some wonderful ponies at homes, farms, and riding schools.

Before writing Pony Pals I wrote fourteen novels for children and young adults. Four of these were honored by Children's Choice Awards.

I live in Sharon, Connecticut, with my husband, Lee, and our dog, Willie. Our daughter is all grown up and has her own apartment in New York City.

Besides writing novels I like to draw, paint, garden, and swim. I didn't have a pony when I was growing up, but I have always loved them and dreamt about riding. Now I take riding lessons on a horse named Saz.

I like reading and writing about ponies as much as I do riding. Which proves to me that you don't have to ride a pony to love them. And you certainly don't need a pony to be a Pony Pal.

Happy Reading,

Jeanne Betancourt

# Pony Pals

### Be a Pony Pal®!

# LITTLE 🍎 APPLE®

# Here are some of our favorite Little Apples.

*Once you take a bite out of a Little Apple book—you'll want to read more!*

**Books for Kids with BIG Appetites!**

- ❏ NA45899-X **Amber Brown Is Not a Crayon**
  Paula Danziger . . . . . . . . . . . . . . . . . . . . . . . . . . . .**$2.99**
- ❏ NA42833-0 **Catwings** Ursula K. LeGuin . . . . . . . . . . . . . . .**$3.50**
- ❏ NA42832-2 **Catwings Return** Ursula K. LeGuin . . . . . . . . . .**$3.50**
- ❏ NA41821-1 **Class Clown** Johanna Hurwitz . . . . . . . . . . . . . .**$3.50**
- ❏ NA42400-9 **Five True Horse Stories** Margaret Davidson . . . . .**$3.50**
- ❏ NA42401-7 **Five True Dog Stories** Margaret Davidson . . . . . .**$3.50**
- ❏ NA43868-9 **The Haunting of Grade Three**
  Grace Maccarone . . . . . . . . . . . . . . . . . . . . . . . . . .**$3.50**
- ❏ NA40966-2 **Rent a Third Grader** B.B. Hiller . . . . . . . . . . . .**$3.50**
- ❏ NA41944-7 **The Return of the Third Grade Ghost Hunters**
  Grace Maccarone . . . . . . . . . . . . . . . . . . . . . . . . . .**$2.99**
- ❏ NA47463-4 **Second Grade Friends** Miriam Cohen . . . . . . .**$3.50**
- ❏ NA45729-2 **Striped Ice Cream** Joan M. Lexau . . . . . . . . . . .**$3.50**

**Available wherever you buy books...or use the coupon below.**

------------------------------------------------------------

# THE *Berenstain* BEAR® SCOUTS

### by Stan & Jan Berenstain

Join Scouts Brother, Sister, Fred, and Lizzy as they defend the weak, catch the crooked, joust against the unjust, and rally against rottenness of all kinds!

| | | |
|---|---|---|
| ☐ BBF60384-1 | The Berenstain Bear Scouts and the Coughing Catfish | $2.99 |
| ☐ BBF60380-9 | The Berenstain Bear Scouts and the Humongous Pumpkin | $2.99 |
| ☐ BBF60385-X | The Berenstain Bear Scouts and the Sci-Fi Pizza | $2.99 |
| ☐ BBF94473-8 | The Berenstain Bear Scouts and the Sinister Smoke Ring | $3.50 |
| ☐ BBF60383-3 | The Berenstain Bear Scouts and the Terrible Talking Termite | $2.99 |
| ☐ BBF60386-8 | The Berenstain Bear Scouts Ghost Versus Ghost | $2.99 |
| ☐ BBF60379-5 | The Berenstain Bear Scouts in Giant Bat Cave | $2.99 |
| ☐ BBF60381-7 | The Berenstain Bear Scouts Meet Bigpaw | $2.99 |
| ☐ BBF60382-5 | The Berenstain Bear Scouts Save That Backscratcher | $2.99 |
| ☐ BBF94475-4 | The Berenstain Bear Scouts and the Magic Crystal Caper | $3.50 |
| ☐ BBF94477-0 | The Berenstain Bear Scouts and the Run-Amuck Robot | $3.50 |
| ☐ BBF94479-7 | The Berenstain Bear Scouts and the Ice Monster | $3.50 |
| ☐ BBF94481-9 | The Berenstain Bear Scouts and the Really Big Disaster | $3.50 |
| ☐ BBF94484-3 | The Berenstain Bear Scouts Scream Their Heads Off | $3.50 |
| ☐ BBF94488-6 | The Berenstain Bear Scouts and the Evil Eye | $3.50 |

© 1998 Berenstain Enterprises, Inc.

*Available wherever you buy books or use this order form.*

Send orders to:
Scholastic Inc., P.O. Box 7502, Jefferson City, MO 65102-7502

Please send me the books I have checked above. I am enclosing $_____ (please add $2.00 to cover shipping and handling). Send check or money order — no cash or C.O.D.s please.

Name _____ Birthdate ___/___/___
                                                                   M   D   Y

Address _____

City _____ State _____ Zip _____